MYSTERY ON THE DOCKS

by THACHER HURD

Harper & Row, Publishers

Mystery on the Docks
Copyright © 1983 by Thacher Hurd
All rights reserved. No part of this book may be
used or reproduced in any manner whatsoever without
written permission except in the case of brief quotations
embodied in critical articles and reviews. Printed in
the United States of America. For information address
Harper & Row, Publishers, Inc., 10 East 53rd Street,
New York, N.Y. 10022. Published simultaneously in
Canada by Fitzhenry & Whiteside Limited, Toronto.
First Edition

Library of Congress Cataloging in Publication Data
Hurd, Thacher.
    Mystery on the docks.
    Summary: Ralph, a short order cook, rescues a
kidnapped opera singer from Big Al and his gang of
nasty rats.
    [1. Mystery and detective stories]   I. Title.
PZ7.H9562My 1983   [E]   82-48261
ISBN 0-06-022701-X
ISBN 0-06-022702-8 (lib. bdg.)

For Nicholas

Ralph, the short-order cook
at the diner on Pier 46,
was washing up for the night.
He sang as he washed.
Ralph loved to sing.

On his nights off
Ralph headed for the opera house
to hear the stars sing, or
he strolled to the end of Pier 46,
playing the accordion
and singing to the stars in the sky.

But tonight there were no stars.
A cold and clammy fog crept over the docks.
A foghorn blew.
The pier creaked.
Then all was quiet.

...Or was it?

Ralph stopped singing.
He heard a ship's engines throbbing.
He saw a dark ship gliding to the dock.
THUD! He heard a gangplank fall.

Two rats slunk out of the gloom.
They headed straight for Ralph's diner.

"Fish and fries!" snapped the shorter rat.

"Right-o," said Ralph. "You work on the dark ship?"

"None of your business," snarled the taller rat.

"Hmmmmmm," thought Ralph, "tough customers."

While the rats gobbled their food,
Ralph read the newspaper.
Suddenly a headline caught his eye:

Singer Mysteriously Vanishes!

RATVILLE, May 16 — The day before his gala concert at the opera house, Eduardo Bombasto—whose thundering voice is known to concertgoers throughout the world—disappeared under mysterious circumstances. The police have no clues.

"Oh, no!" cried Ralph.
"My favorite singer is missing!"
BAM! The diner door slammed.
Ralph whirled around.

The two rats were gone!
"Hey, come back here!" Ralph yelled. "Pay up!"
But the pier was empty.

. . . Or was it?

Suddenly, a car screeched to a stop
in front of the dark ship.
Three rats jumped out.
Ralph hid behind a crate.

"Okay, boys! Get the sack out of the trunk!"
shouted a huge rat chomping a cigar.
"Right, Big Al!"

Ralph tiptoed closer.
CRASH! He tripped on a rope.
"Catch him! Snatch him!" yelled Big Al.
Ralph scampered down the pier.

But the rats
were too quick
on their paws.
"Throw him in the hold!"
snapped Big Al.

"Welcome aboard!" laughed the same two rats
who hadn't paid for their fish and fries.

The dark ship pulled away from the dock.
Ralph was alone in the hold.

. . . Or was he?

The sack behind Ralph began to wiggle.
"Who's there?" Ralph cried out.

"HELP!"

Ralph untied the sack.
Out popped...Eduardo!

"Who are you?" Eduardo asked suspiciously.
"I'm your biggest fan," replied Ralph.
"What are you doing here?"
"Big Al kidnapped me," said Eduardo.
"I'll walk the plank if he doesn't get his ransom."
"We've got to get off this ship! Fast!" cried Ralph.

Ralph and Eduardo sneaked on deck.
Big Al was on guard.
The night was black as coal.
The ship was far out in the harbor.
"AHA!" yelled Big Al.
"Trying to escape, eh? We'll fix you!"

Ralph and Eduardo ran for it.
Straight up the mast and into the crow's nest.

"Look! Flares!" shouted Ralph.
"We can signal for help!"

"The fog is too thick," said Eduardo.
"The police will never see the flares."
"What else can we do?" said Ralph.

"I can sing!" exclaimed Eduardo.

A police-boat siren wailed in the distance.

"They saw the flares!" cried Ralph.

"NO!" said Eduardo.

"They heard *me* sing!"

Big Al was hopping mad.
"Full steam ahead!" he shouted.
But the dark ship was slow
and the police boat was fast.

"Come out with your hands up!" yelled the police chief.

But Big Al was not about to give up.
He was too tough.
And besides,
he was winning.

...Or was he?

Suddenly two figures swooped down out of the fog.
Ralph and Eduardo to the rescue!
"Rats overboard!" yelled the police chief.

WHAP!

BAM!

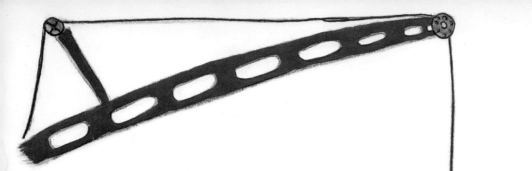

The police fished Big Al and his gang
out of the water.
Their fur was dripping.
Their teeth were chattering.
Their dark ship
was towed back to the pier.
They were towed to jail.

The next day Ralph's picture
was on the front page of the newspaper.
He was a hero!
Eduardo gave him a front-row seat
for his concert at the opera house.

After the concert Ralph invited Eduardo
and all his friends to a party on Pier 46.

The stars were shining brightly.
Ralph played the accordion
and sang for his favorite opera star.
Everyone danced, and munched fish and fries,
and toasted Ralph, who had saved Eduardo
from Big Al and his gang of nasty rats.

W24
LC-712119

Adl-9/11/00
CC-1T

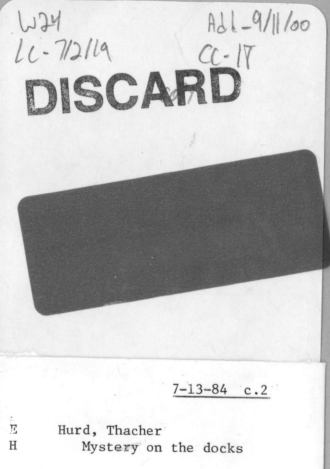

7-13-84 c.2

E   Hurd, Thacher
H   Mystery on the docks